10
Minute Tales

When you see t...

Read aloud
Read aloud to
your child.

Read alon
Support your c
as they read ald

EGMONT
We bring stories to life

It was a sunny morning at the Nursery.
The class had gathered around Osbourne.

Osbourne was holding
three big boxes.

What could be inside?

Timmy and his friends
jumped up and down and
spun around and around!

They were all very excited
and couldn't wait to peep
inside the boxes.

Boxes! What could be inside?

Timmy spied a box with a tractor on the lid. He picked it up and bounced up and down so much, the lid flew open!

Baah!Baah! Timmy bleated. Lots of wooden pieces crashed on to the table.

Timmy stared at the strange shapes. He wondered what they were for.

Timmy chose a box with a tractor on the lid.

Osbourne joined some of the pieces together. They made a picture of some wheels.

Baah! Timmy bleated, happily. Now he understood. It was a jigsaw puzzle! He had to join the pieces together to make a picture.

Soon enough, Timmy had almost finished the puzzle.

But wait . . . there was one piece missing!

Read alone

It was a jigsaw puzzle!
Oh no, one piece was missing.

Read aloud   Read along

Timmy ran outside to look for the missing jigsaw piece.

Paxton was busy playing with a toy train. Maybe it is in there! Timmy thought.

He grabbed the train and shook it hard. Something rattled inside!

But when a little piece of wood fell out, Timmy bleated sadly. It wasn't the missing jigsaw piece.

Timmy found a little piece of wood.
It wasn't the missing jigsaw piece.

Over on the picnic rug, Mittens, Stripey and Otus were enjoying an afternoon tea party.

Timmy marched over to his friends. Maybe they could help Timmy find his jigsaw piece.

Then Timmy spied a blue tea-set box on the rug.

Baah! Timmy bleated.

The jigsaw piece might be hiding in there!

Read alone

Do Timmy's friends have
the missing jigsaw piece?

Read aloud Read along

Timmy picked up the box.
Something bumped up and down inside.

Bump! Bump! Bump!

It must be the missing piece! Timmy thought.

But when he tipped the box upside down,
only a toy key and a plastic flower fell out.

Timmy felt very disappointed.

Read alone

Timmy found a key and a flower
but not the missing puzzle piece.

Just then, the cuckoo clock went off. **CUCKOO!** It was time for the class to go for an afternoon nap. **Zzz!**

Soon, everybody was sleeping peacefully. Everybody except Timmy.

Timmy looked at the objects he had found – a little piece of wood, a key and a flower.

He'd found lots of things but he just wanted to find his missing piece!

Read alone

At nap time, Timmy still hadn't found the missing jigsaw piece.

Read aloud   Read along

Maybe the missing jigsaw piece is under Apricot's pillow! Timmy thought suddenly.

He tiptoed over to Apricot and lifted up her pillow. Poor Apricot let out a surprised **HiCoo** as she rolled on to the floor!

Harriet looked up and let out a loud **Cluck!**

Timmy ran back to his pillow.

He felt sad that he still hadn't found the missing piece. But he couldn't keep his eyes open any longer and soon he was fast asleep.

Timmy looked under Apricot's pillow.

A little later, Harriet clapped her wings to wake up the animals.

One by one, the friends stretched and let out sleepy yawns.

Timmy was still fast asleep.

Suddenly, Otus let out an excited **Toowit toowoo!**

Then Paxton let out a happy **OINK!**

They had found the flower and the key next to Timmy's pillow.

Timmy didn't notice a thing.

Otus and Paxton saw the key
and the flower beside Timmy.

Ruffy skipped over to Timmy's pillow to see what his friends had found.

He jumped up into the air when he saw the little piece of wood on the floor. **Ruff Ruff!**

What could the animals want with Timmy's strange objects?

Read alone

Ruffy barked happily when he found the piece of wood!

Paxton, Otus and Ruffy ran outside with the objects they had found.

Paxton used the key to wind up the little wooden train. It set off with a loud **whirr!**

Then Otus put the flower on top of the teapot. Timmy had found the lid!

The friends were very pleased.

Read alone

The key was for the toy train.
The flower went on the teapot.

Read aloud   Read along

The little piece of wood was for the green boat. Ruffy pulled a string and raised a beautiful blue sail!

Finlay let out a happy **Yip Yap!**

Meanwhile, poor Timmy wasn't quite so happy. He was still looking for his jigsaw piece.

Timmy had found everybody else's missing pieces. Why couldn't he find his own?

Read alone

Ruffy used the little piece of wood as a mast for his boat!

Later that afternoon, when Yabba was clearing away the tea party, something fell out of the teapot.

Plop! It was Timmy's missing jigsaw piece!

The animals jumped up and down in excitement!

Then they had a clever idea.

Yabba placed the piece into the train carriage. Then Paxton wound up the train with his key.

Read alone

Then the friends found Timmy's jigsaw piece in the teapot!

Read aloud   Read along

The train whizzed over the lawn
and through the Nursery door.

It bumped into the table with a loud **CRASH!**

Baah! Timmy bleated in surprise.

The jigsaw piece flew up into the air.
It was heading straight for Timmy!

Timmy quickly moved out of the way and
the piece landed in the hole of the jigsaw!

Read alone

They put the piece in the train.
It whizzed through the Nursery.

Read aloud   Read along

The jigsaw was done! It was a lovely picture of a red and orange tractor.

Timmy was very proud to have finished his jigsaw puzzle.

And he was pleased that he had helped his friends find their missing pieces, too!

Read alone

The jigsaw was done! It was a
picture of a red and orange tractor.

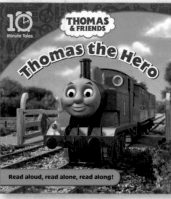

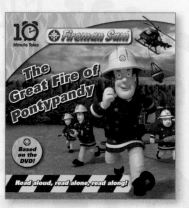